W9-CSI-971

# YOUR DINOCREW

**BOSUN**
Stegosaurus

**CAPTAIN**
Hadrosaurus

**CABIN BOY**
Tyrannosaurus rex

# DINOSAILORS

## DEB LUND

Illustrated by

## HOWARD FINE

**Voyager Books • Harcourt, Inc.**

Orlando • Austin • New York • San Diego • Toronto • London

www.HarcourtBooks.com

First Voyager Books edition 2008

*Voyager Books* is a trademark of Harcourt, Inc.,
registered in the United States of America and/or other jurisdictions.

The Library of Congress has cataloged the hardcover edition as follows:
Lund, Deb.
Dinosailors/Deb Lund; illustrated by Howard Fine.
p.   cm.
Summary: After spending time sailing, some seasick dinosaurs decide
they have had enough of the high seas.
[ 1. Dinosaurs—Fiction.    2. Sailing—Fiction.    3. Stories in rhyme.]
I. Fine, Howard, ill.    II. Title.
PZ8.3.L9715Di   2003
[E]—dc21      2002011591
ISBN 978-0-15-204609-5
ISBN 978-0-15-206124-1 pb


TWP    C  E  G  H  F  D  B


The illustrations in this book were done in gouache and watercolors.
Title calligraphy by Tom Seibert.
The text type was set in Bryn Mawr.
Color separations by Colourscan Co. Pte. Ltd., Singapore
Printed in Singapore by Tien Wah Press Pte. Ltd.
Production supervision by Christine Witnik
Designed by Ivan Holmes

For Uncle Vern and the Shifty Sailors
—D. L.

For Bo and Rhino
—H. F.

**D**inosailors at the slip
Cry out, "Ahoy!" and board their ship.
They swab the deck, stow dinogear,
Ignoring clouds that linger near.

They're hale and hearty—dinotough!
They talk of salty sailing stuff:
Blocks and winches, dinocleats,
Shackles, tacking, trimming sheets.

Dinosailors choose a course,
Raise anchor using dinoforce.
They haul on lines, hoist dinosails,
And scale the rigging with their tails.

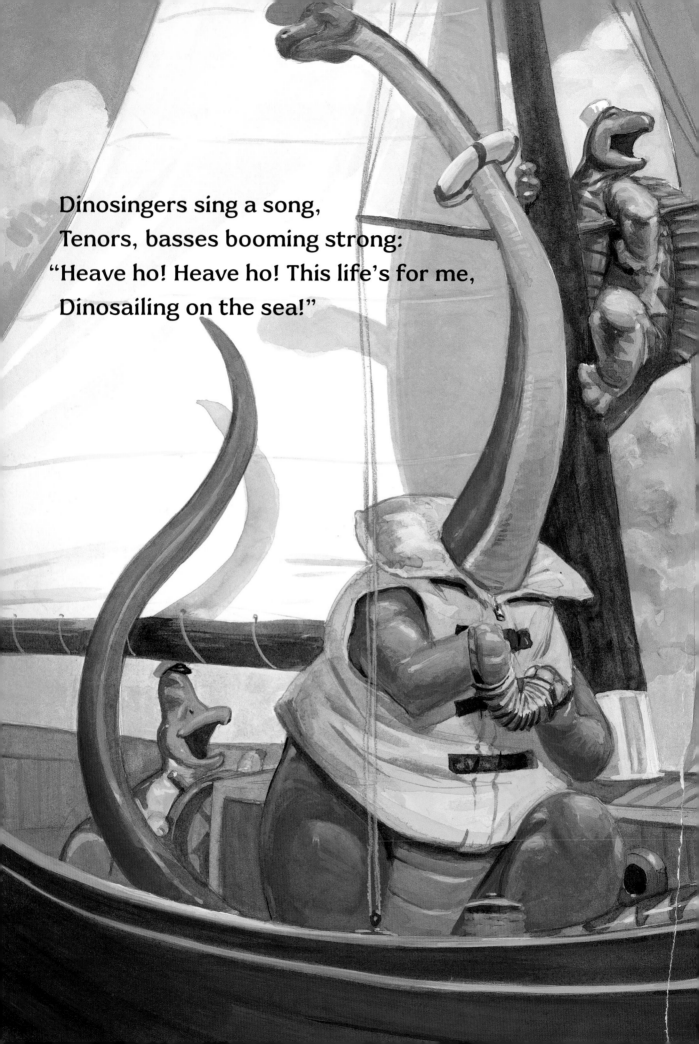

Dinosingers sing a song,
Tenors, basses booming strong:
"Heave ho! Heave ho! This life's for me,
Dinosailing on the sea!"

Dinosailors have a ball,
Until their vessel hits a squall.
The water tosses all around.
Their dinofeet miss solid ground.

They dinosault like Ping-Pong balls,
Bumping dinorumps and walls.
Dinoswingers hang from sails.
They mash the mast and ram the rails.

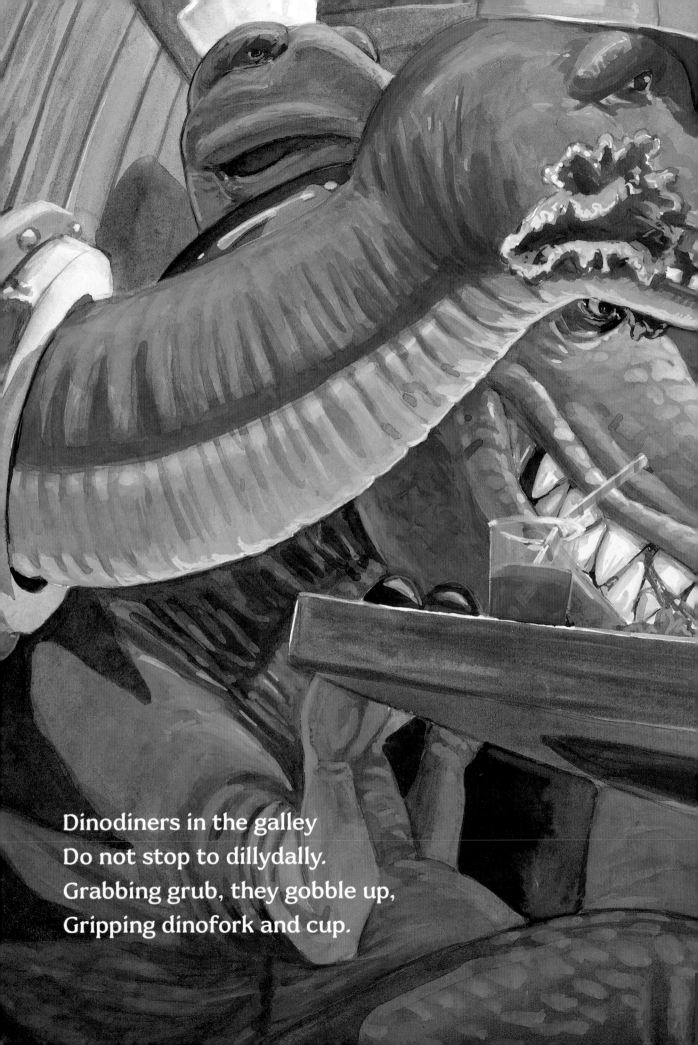

Dinodiners in the galley
Do not stop to dillydally.
Grabbing grub, they gobble up,
Gripping dinofork and cup.

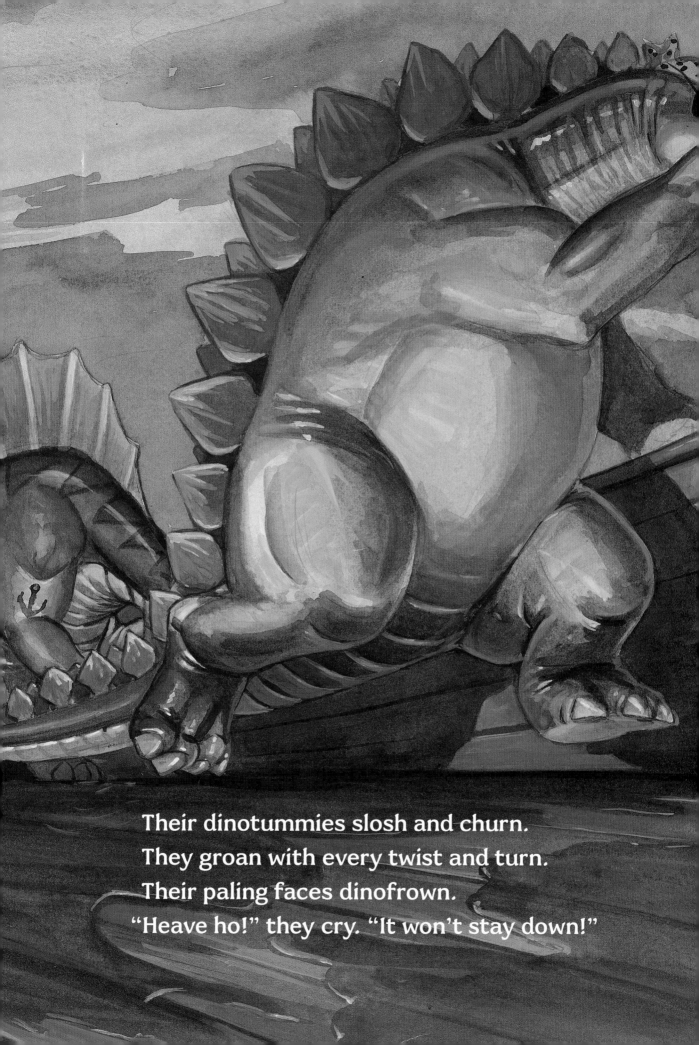

Their dinotummies slosh and churn.
They groan with every twist and turn.
Their paling faces dinofrown.
"Heave ho!" they cry. "It won't stay down!"

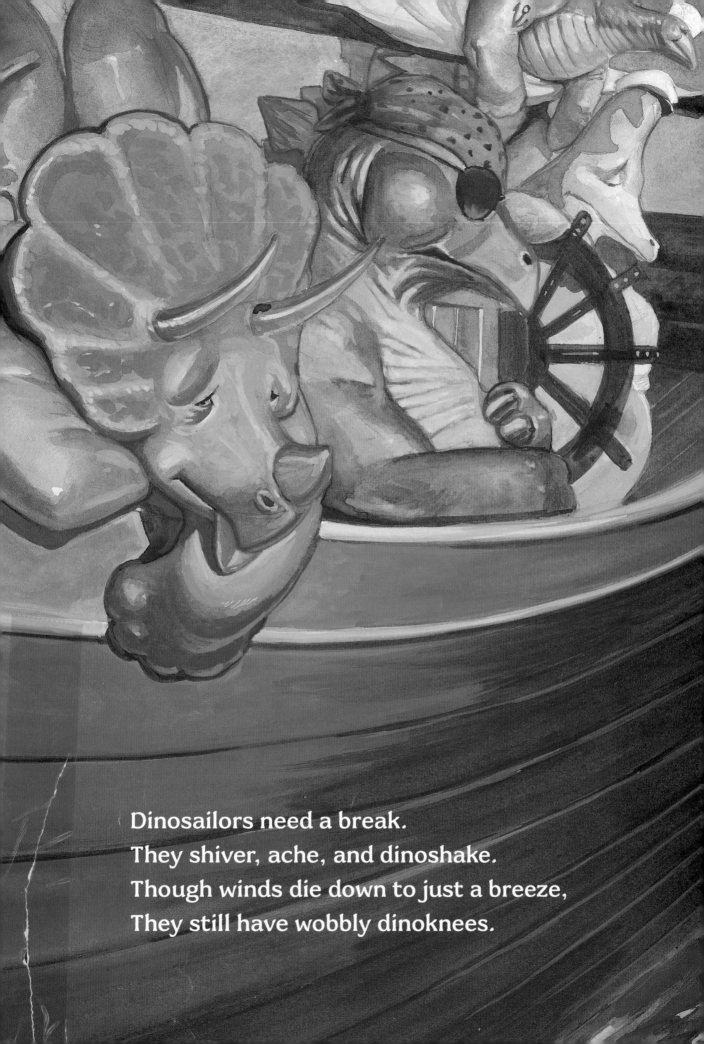

Dinosailors need a break.
They shiver, ache, and dinoshake.
Though winds die down to just a breeze,
They still have wobbly dinoknees.

The woozy dinos moan and weep.
The day's been long—they need some sleep.
In dinojammies at the head,
They brush and floss, then climb in bed.

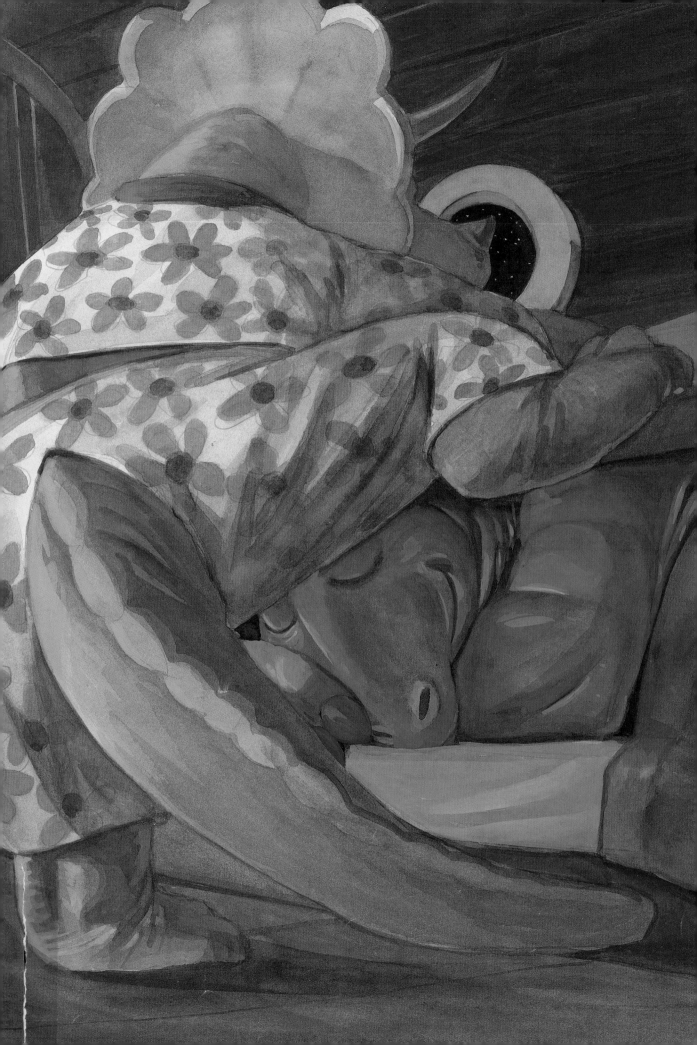

When they awake, they cry, "No more!"
"We're sick of decks—we want a floor!"

Dinowhiners reach the land
And stagger off, so glad to stand.

Dinosailors sell that boat.
They'd rather dinostroll than float.
They go back home to those they miss,
To cuddle, hug, and dinokiss.

This dinolife is calm and slow,
For dinos who were on the go.
Once more they hear adventure's cry,
So dinotravelers say good-bye.

No more a seasick dinobunch,
They find a way to keep their lunch.
In harmony, they join the chord . . .

"Dinotrainers, all aboard!"

# YOUR DINOCREW

**FIRST MATE**
Spinosaurus

**DECKHAND**
Brachiosaurus

**SECOND MATE**
Triceratops